The Truth About
Three Billy Goats Gruff

AS TOLD TO
STEVEN OTFINOSKI

PICTURES BY
ROWAN BARNES–MURPHY

Troll Associates

Library of Congress Cataloging-in-Publication Data

Otfinoski, Steven.
The truth about three billy goats Gruff / as told to Steven
Otfinoski; pictures by Rowan Barnes-Murphy.
p.   cm.
Summary: The troll tells his own version of what happened when
three billy goats named Billy, Bill, and William Gruff tried to
cross his bridge.
ISBN 0-8167-3013-X (pbk.)
[1. Trolls—Fiction. 2. Goats—Fiction.] I. Barnes-Murphy,
Rowan, ill. II. Asbjornsen, Peter Christen, 1812-1885. Tre bukkene
Bruse. III. Title.
PZ7.O876Tr 1994
[E]—dc20   93-42391

Published by Troll Associates, Inc.
WhistleStop is a trademark of Troll Associates.

Printed in the United States of America.

10 9 8 7 6 5 4 3 2 1

The name is Troll. Tobias T. Troll. I know what you're thinking. Trolls are big, ugly, and mean. Well, I am big and I suppose I wouldn't win any beauty contests. But mean? Why, I'm the sweetest guy you could ever meet. That is, I was until those three awful Goats Gruff came along.

It all started one day while I was taking my daily snooze under my bridge. I call it *my* bridge because I built it stone by stone with my own hands. I live under the bridge so I can collect tolls from anyone who wants to cross it. You might call me a toll troll. It's not a bad way to make a living.

Anyway, I was taking my daily nap when I was suddenly awakened by this TRIP! TRAP! TRIP! TRAP! sound on the bridge.

"Aha!" I said to myself. "A customer!"

I peered up from under my bridge and found myself face to face with a scrawny little goat.

"That'll be five cents, please," I said politely.

"Five cents for what?" he asked.

"Five cents for crossing *my* bridge," I told him.

"*Your* bridge?" answered the goat.

"Yes," I said. "I'm the toll troll."

"I don't care if you're the Easter Bunny," replied the goat gruffly. "I'm Billy Goat Gruff and I'm not paying you one cent. I just want to get to that hillside over there and munch on the nice green grass."

I didn't like his tone of voice at all, but I remained calm and reasonable.

"I'm afraid you'll have to pay me first if you want to get to the hillside from this bridge," I said.

Billy Goat Gruff stroked his little white beard while he thought.

"I'll tell you what," he said at last. "My big brother Bill is not far behind me. He's got enough money to pay the toll for both of us. You can collect the money from him. Okay?"

Now I didn't trust this Billy Goat Gruff. Not at all. He had shifty eyes. But he was the scrawniest goat I'd ever seen. He needed fattening up in the worst way. So against my better judgment, I let the little goat cross my bridge without paying.

Soon I was settled back under the bridge, snoring away. TRIP! TRAP! TRIP! TRAP! Again I was awakened. I didn't need to look to know who it was. If you've heard one goat TRIP! TRAP! you've heard them all.

"Is that Bill Goat Gruff, big brother of Billy Goat Gruff, who passed by here a while ago?" I yelled out.

"And just who wants to know?" asked the goat in a gruff voice.

"I do," I said, as I poked my head up from under the bridge and smiled.

"Why, you're nothing but an old, ugly troll," said Bill Goat Gruff, who was considerably bigger than his brother. He had tiny red eyes and two small horns on the top of his snow-white head.

I ignored this remark. "I'm afraid you owe me ten cents," I explained. "This is a toll bridge. You must

pay me five cents for yourself and five cents for your brother Billy, who had no money."

Bill Goat Gruff just snickered. "Do you think I carry loose change on me when I'm on my way to the hillside to stuff my face with grass?" he said. "Get serious, Troll."

Well, I thought I *was* being serious. But apparently this ill-mannered goat didn't think so.

"Look," I said. "This is *my* bridge. If you want to cross it, you'll have to pay up, just like everyone else."

Bill Goat Gruff scratched his long, thin beard as he thought.

"The goat you want to talk to is my big brother William," he said after a while. "He's on his way here right now, and he's got plenty of money. He'll pay you for all three of us and throw in a hefty tip, too."

Now I didn't trust Bill Goat Gruff any more than I did his little brother. But he did look awfully hungry. "Okay," I sighed. "You can cross my bridge. But you'd better be telling the truth about your brother William."

"He'll be here any minute," said Bill Goat Gruff. "Honest."

Suddenly a terrible thought came to me. "Tell me," I asked Bill Goat Gruff, "do you have any other brothers besides Billy and William?" I didn't want to go broke letting a huge family of goats cross my bridge for free.

"Nope," said Bill Goat Gruff. "There's just the three of us. See you around."

With that, he passed across the bridge and headed straight for the green, grassy hillside.

This time I didn't lie down under the bridge for a nap. I sat right in the middle of the bridge with my eyes wide open and waited for William Goat Gruff. I didn't have to wait long.

TRIP! TRAP! TRIP! TRAP! came his heavy hoofs on the road. There he was, the biggest goat of them all, just as Bill Goat Gruff had said. William Goat Gruff had two large, curved horns on the top of his head. He looked mean.

But that didn't scare me one bit. I was determined to get my money, one way or another.

"Hold it right there," I said before he set one hoof on my bridge. "Are you William Goat Gruff?"

"That's right," said the goat gruffly. "Now out of my way, you ugly troll. I'm late for a lunch date with my two brothers."

"That's what I want to talk to you about," I said. "Your two brothers couldn't pay me the toll to cross my bridge, and they said you would pay it for them."

William Goat Gruff tugged at his thick, scraggly beard.

"Isn't that just like those two moochers to leave me with the tab!" he cried. "All right, what do I owe you?"

"Fifteen cents," I said.

"What?" cried William Goat Gruff. "Fifteen cents to cross this crummy little bridge? Why, that's highway robbery!"

Now even trolls have tempers, and when he called my bridge crummy and little, I got really mad.

"That's enough," I said. "Now pay up or you can

just turn around and go right back where you came from!"

William Goat Gruff gave me a nasty grin. "And what if I don't?" he asked.

This was really too much! "If you don't," I sputtered, "I'll, I'll—"

"You'll *what*?" asked the goat.

"I'll gobble you up!" I cried.

It was a poor choice of words. I had no intention of eating William Goat Gruff. The truth is, I've never touched goat meat.

SCRAPE
SCRAPE

William Goat Gruff must have seen I was bluffing. He scraped his hoofs on the bridge and lowered his horns.

"Just try to gobble me, Troll!" he challenged. "I'll send you on a one-way trip to the moon!"

What could I do? It was a matter of pride as well as money. Besides, I was hopping mad. I prepared to defend myself.

Now this is the part of the story where William Goat Gruff is supposed to have butted me right off the bridge. But don't you believe it! It didn't happen that way at all.

Here's what really happened. Just as the goat was coming for me, a farmer came rumbling down the road with a wagonload of hay. He took one look at us and thought I was attacking the goat.

The farmer raced for the bridge and yelled, "Leave that poor little goat alone, you big, bad troll!"

Boy, did he have it wrong! He was so excited that he lost control of his horse. His wagon was about to run right over me. I leaped off the bridge just in time.

I landed with a crash on the rocks at the bottom of the river. Ooh! Did that hurt! The swirling waters tossed me this way and that. I was carried by the rushing current about half a mile downriver. Then I grabbed hold of a piece of driftwood that had lodged itself on a rock and hung on for dear life.

Two boys who were fishing on the shore saw me. They pulled me out of the water and called for help. To make a long story short, I spent two weeks in the hospital with three broken ribs and a fractured elbow.

When I finally mended, I went straight home. And do you know what I found? Those three Goats Gruff—Billy, Bill, and William—had taken over my bridge! They had put in a fancy gate, a tollbooth, and a salad bar. And do you know what they were charging people to cross the bridge? Twenty cents!

It just goes to show you what happens when you
try to be nice to hungry goats. They walk all over you!